This book is for my beautiful children, Fox and Ever.

Be proud to be who you are, no matter what, and be kind to others!

Daddy loves you so much.

—Benji.

For my three mighty cubs, Eva, Jesse and Heath.– James

To my friend with the heart of a warrior, Sam – Rory

Published by Scholastic Australia in 2024.

Edited by Michelle Lee, Gabrielle Read and Hannah Francis
Designed by Will Harrison-Smith and Hannah Francis

Scholastic Australia Pty Limited
PO Box 579 Gosford NSW 2250
ABN 11 000 614 577
www.scholastic.com.au

Part of the Scholastic Group
Sydney * Auckland * New York * Toronto * London * Mexico City
New Delhi * Hong Kong * Buenos Aires * Puerto Rico

ISBN 978-1-76152-703-6

Printed in China.

Scholastic Australia's policy, in association with its printers, is to use papers that are renewable and made efficiently from wood grown in responsibly managed forests, so as to minimise its environmental footprint.

NATIONAL LIBRARY OF AUSTRALIA
A catalogue record for this book is available from the National Library of Australia

BENJI MARSHALL

HEART OF A TIGER

WITH RORY H. MATHER

ILLUSTRATED BY JAMES HART

SCHOLASTIC
SYDNEY AUCKLAND NEW YORK TORONTO LONDON MEXICO CITY
NEW DELHI HONG KONG BUENOS AIRES PUERTO RICO

Ty was a tiger
unlike any other.
He wasn't loud like his sister
or strong like his brother.

He could run, he could jump,
he could pounce, he could crawl.
But he had **no stripes.**
Not one, none at all.

He tried to fit in
but, try as he might,
no stripes on a tiger?
Just didn't feel right.

Ty had to try
something,
by hook or by crook.

He came up with a plan
to try change his look.

Ty now had stripes,

he was a tiger at last!

But when he went near his family,
they ran away fast.

‘Check out my stripes!
What do you think?’

‘Go away, Ty!’
‘My goodness, **you stink.**’

So, Ty then decided,
to try something **new.**
'I'll tie on some vines.
Yes, that's what I'll do.'

When he next saw his family,
he was covered in **plants!**
They thought he was dancing
until he yelled...

AAN

Ty refused to give up,
by **hook** or
by **crook.**

He was determined
to add **stripes**
to his look!

JUNGLE INK
OPEN
NO CUBS ALLOWED!

But after so many tries,
Ty curled up in a ball.
And he said to himself,
'I'm no tiger at all.'

As he sat feeling sad,
Ty heard a cry...

'HELP US, WE'RE STUCK!'
'OH, PLEASE HELP US, TY.'

Ty sprang into action, grabbing his vine.
He swung it and roared:

Ty refused to give up,
by hook or by crook,
he'd save all his siblings—
whatever it took.

With one final tug,
at last, they were free.
'Ty, you're so strong!'
'And you **roared** just like me!'

From that day on,
Ty forgot about stripes.
For when it comes to **tigers**,
there are many types.

Some tigers have stripes,
some tigers can roar...

But what's in your **heart?**
That matters much more.